INCONGRUENT FLAMINGO

S
C

If it has three legs, then you know it isn't real . . .

INCONGRUENT FLAMINGO

contents

Cat and Crow

Remy Nakamura

Cat and Crow were friends.

Crow was one of those uncommon crows who spoke English. She wielded words as weapons, riling up crowds on the streets of Hollywood the way she poked with a twig at sand piles to make them swarm with biting red ants. Everyone knew that crows were priests (or more technically, tour guides for the newly dead), but Crow liked to think of herself as something more—a black-winged avatar of Chaos. She kept things interesting for all beings, be they silly bipeds or spicy insect bites.

Like many corvids, her favorite word was Fuck. It tasted and felt just right: the way it started life deep in her gullet, how she bit it off at the end, like slicing a grub in half. Fuuuuck she'd say, instantly delighting as hairy human heads turned this way and that in confused accusation. Sometimes she tacked on a "you" like a fledgling chasing after its parent. Crow always had fucks to give. She was generous like that.

Cat could also talk, but they kept mostly silent. Shapeshifting was more Cat's thing than talking, anyway. Cat often took the shape of a tall, sleek human of ambiguous race and androgynous appearance. Like Crow, Cat found humans compelling. Unlike Crow, Cat liked humans.

Crow thought Cat was a slut, and told them so, partly because she liked the word, and also because Cat fucked a lot of humans. Because Cat was beautiful and had grey irises like quiet storms and listened way more than they spoke, they found no lack of partners. Cat had a dexterous tongue, all cunning linguist tossing salads and playing woodwinds and leaving in their wake a long and languorous list of satisfied lovers.

Crows and cats more generally are not known for interspecies camaraderie, but these two shared an affinity for fucking/with humans, and they met at an aromatic dumpster full of end of day fish and chips across from the Hollywood Forever Cemetery. A plastic pink flamingo perched near a gravestone in the corner, staring at them with one eye. Cat would meet in cat form, licking their black fur to a shine.

"Cat," Crow might caw. "Cat! Don't fuck humans, or they'll fuck you. Over! I'm call!ing you out."

After a long, thoughtful pause, Cat might reply, "Humans are irresistible." They purred all of their 'r's, rolling them around like a cat in sunshine. "They're scrumptious, like cream, like kippered herring."

"Gah! Fuck! Yuck!" Crow might say.

"Oh," Cat might reply, in an uncharacteristic verbal flood: "Not just flavor. Touch and sound, sight and thought. They write words, on paperrr. Carefully crafted stories. And philosophies! Have you heard of Camus? *The Myth of Sisyphus*. He forever rolls a rock up a knoll."

"Fuck rocks!"

"Camus swears this man is content. Maybe humans are my rock to roll."

One day, at the intersection of Hollywood and Highland, Cat the human was crushed by a pink Cadillac with a chrome flamingo hood ornament and a well-known celebrity driver. The car screeched away, leaving Cat the cat behind on the curb, bloody and broken, and Crow, bereaved.

Crow mourned in the way that crows mourn, summoning a vast murder made of every capable crow between the mountains and the sea and the OC suburbs. Like the professional mourners that they were, they wore black and cast their heads back calling and crying out in cacophonous contagious communal desolation and lamentation. In their rage, they carpeted all below with f-bombs and shit-bombs.

Later, Crow met Cat's spirit, in human shape, and they moved along in silence down Santa Monica Boulevard. They stopped shy of the 405, in front of the obscenely huge Mormon Temple, which sat on top of an open, grassy hill that wasn't a golf course. A half-dozen flamingos were perched here and there, perhaps fake, perhaps not. A vehicular ruin was poised at the bottom, nose pointed up, waiting.

"How about here," Cat asked.

"Fuck me," Crow said, thoughtfully.

Cat stared at Crow for a bit, then leaned into the wreck, pushing it inch by inch up the slope.

HOA

Jeb R. Sherrill

"That's *not* a flamingo?" I asked, standing with my brother in the front yard, staring at the biggest *not flamingo* I'd ever seen. It stood in the flower bed, but its head reached the second story. The gaping maw lay frozen in time, daring us to step closer.

"No," said Gary with a pride usually reserved for the deformed two-headed snowmen he created every Christmas. "It's technically a crane, spray painted pink."

I twisted up my mouth. The gargantuan effigy towered over the yard like some prehistoric colossus dredged from the deep and distant past, come to devour hapless intruders. "Seems like it might play fast and loose with the letter of the HOA laws," I said, impressed by how lifelike the bird might have appeared if Gary hadn't added an aviator hat and hubcap goggles to the creature.

My brother folded his arms. "The Homeowners Association strictly stipulates *flamingos*. It says nothing about cranes, Article 25, Section 6B."

I rolled my eyes and glanced down the street, knowing full well Mildred the neighborhood narc had probably already taken a myriad of snapshots with her telephoto lens and sent them to the proper authorities. "You know mom's in there crying?" I said, wondering how Gary could stand to wear his signature knit cap with white fluffy balls on the sides in the middle of summer.

"She'll be fine," Gary said. His grin stretched from ear to ear. I knew the image of Mildred furiously dialing her phone, rage spreading across her cheeks, was probably giving him more satisfaction than a woman of her age should. "Mom hates that old bag anyway."

She *did* hate Mildred almost as much as she hated the Homeowners Association, but she feared them even more. Gary had antagonized the hapless organization out of pure spite by filling the entire front yard with no less than four hundred and fifty-two pink flamingos the year before. Needless to say, his rash actions had necessitated the rules being changed to not only ban the hated neon lawn fowl, but added a fine for such egregious infractions of no less than $5,000 per flamingo and expulsion from all block parties for life.

"And Mom hates block parties," Gary said, reading my mind.

I squinted at the oddly shaped beak. It might have been a barbeque grill at one time, but my brother had twisted it well out of recognition. "Did you weld that?"

Gary nodded. "The wings are car doors from a Lamborghini I found in a junk yard."

Shaking my head, I stifled a laugh. "If anyone sees that at night, they're going to piss themselves."

"Dad already did," Gary said. "He tried to rip the poor fella out, but the feet are rebarred into six feet of concrete."

"Can rebar be verbed?"

"Can verb be verbed?" Gary asked with a sideways smirk.

And that was that. Once my brother had a stupid idea, the best the rest of us could do was roll our eyes, grin, and bear it. A dead stillness settled over the house. Mom spent most of the time sobbing as she rewashed the same dish for forty-five minutes straight and dad paced a trench in the carpet.

I sat trying to look calm while Gary peered through blinds out at the neighborhood with the type of glee usually reserved for Amazon delivery drivers. Sweat dripped beneath my arms. Dad had once cut the hedges an inch and a half too high, prompting both a $500 fine and threats to have him beheaded in the central gazebo.

We had already been fined for having a fence too high, then having a fence too low, then simply for having a fence. Our shed in the back had been flagged for having an overly shiny roof. Mom's prized birdfeeder had been confiscated for attracting squirrels. Dad's truck had been marked for *being a truck* and I had been fined twice my college tuition for sleeping in my car in the driveway. I had actually been trying to extricate a cassette from under the springs of the passenger seat for two and a half hours.

Mom shrieked out of nowhere. "Did you wash the sidewalk?"

Dad stopped pacing and narrowed his eyes. "Pretty sure. And Rick left a bag of wet grass around the side of the house, but I got rid of it," he said giving me the stink-eye before resuming his pacing.

"They could take the house. Confiscate our vehicles. Send us to prison," Mom wailed. "They could have us executed."

I stifled a gulp. She wasn't wrong. Old Man Bernard had been shot in the head in front of his family for parking on the street one day and his wife had been fined for the mess his body left on the sidewalk.

"Dammit, Ger, can't you just take it down?" I shouted. "If I have to re-paint the house one more time this month, my pants are going to be whiter than the tulips."

He glared at me. "You know I can't do that."

I knew. His war with the Homeowners Association went back years. Half the restrictions in the bylaws had been written because of our house, and all the most interesting infractions had been mine and Gary's. Like the time we'd filled an inflatable bounce house with Mentos and lobbed Diet Coke-filled balloons at it from the roof. Or the time we'd sprayed the shrubs with blue flocking. Or the steam train we'd set up on the roof with no holiday within a thirty-day period to cover the *decorations* clause. Or the spotlight we'd set up on the roof as a security light. It hadn't been our fault its mechanical roving not only crossed Mildred's front window but may or may not have been programmed to linger there just long enough to give anyone on the couch second degree burns.

If April Fool's Day had been a recognized holiday, we might have gotten away with our toilet paper cascading waterfall. But the look on their faces had been well worth it as the cataract of mega rolls bounding down into the street had disrupted traffic for an evening.

But the HOA was above the law and Gary's war with them knew no bounds. He'd tested the grey areas of every article and ordinance they'd ever written, including the ones which somehow named him specifically. He'd gone by Larry for six months just so he could write his name on Mildred's lawn in gasoline without incurring a fine. Bet they wish they'd worded that rule a little different.

The doorbell rang. Our eyes shot to front door.

"You expecting anything?" Dad asked the room.

We shook our heads.

The doorbell rang again.

Dad balled his fists next to his sides. A man's home was his castle, and it was his job to answer the door. We watched with pity as he hung his head and trudged forwards. The bell blared again as he reached for the knob. I swear the damned thing kept getting louder.

"There's no hope for you this time," Mildred snapped, her steel eyes poking holes through to the back of Dad's head. "That flamingo of yours is scaring children."

"It's a heron," Gary hollered over Dad's shoulder. Article 45, Section 22."

Dad hadn't taken his eyes off our intruder. He also hadn't moved to let her step across the threshold. "Boy says it's a heron," he said, sweat streaming down the back of his neck.

"Thought you said it was a crane," I whispered to Gary.

"Tomato potato," he whispered back with a one-shoulder shrug.

She took a labored breath beneath her orange sundress. "Can you *prove* that's not a flamingo?" Mildred sneered.

Dad wasn't giving an inch, but his knees looked like they were trying to buckle. "Any way you can prove it *is* a flamingo?"

They stared at each other for a period only two years shorter than the last ice age.

Dad swallowed.

Mildred gave a harsh sniff.

"Well, you have a good day," Dad said.

The older woman wet her lips. "Your family is going down." Her soft mid-western accent cut through the room like an overcharged light saber.

She turned on her heel and stomped away with her nose so far in the air a light rain would have drowned her.

Dad shut the door with a quivering hand and sank against it. "They're gonna kill us."

"Shit," I said.

Gary whimpered a little, but I couldn't be sure if he was laughing or crying. He stared at the carpet, having to know he'd pushed it too far this time.

The flick-flicking of a sprinkler broke the dead silence. "How long has the sprinkler been on?" Mom asked.

Dad's face went a little white. "Over twenty minutes."

Sprinting for the dining room, I made an almost-elegant dive roll out an open window. Landing in a less-than-graceful staggering flop I stumbled towards the spigot and twisted the valve.

A black drone whizzed over my head.

"Shit," I snapped, scrambling back through the window. "Gary, net gun!" I shouted.

Gary had wasted no time dropping to one knee and throwing another window open. He aimed out into the yard like a duck hunter scanning for clay pigeons.

"They'll already have the video," Dad said, his voice a rasping whisper. "They'll have seen the spray. We're goners."

"Not necessarily," Gary said without turning his head. He squeezed the trigger and a flittering whisper launched out the window followed moments later by a soft thud. "Cheap bastards. No way they're buying anything that sends video."

We followed him out the back door as he power-walked towards the downed prey. He knelt by the contraption, turning it over his hands. "Cheap shit. Wal-Mart. There's an SD card," he said, flipping open a plastic flap and pulling forth a little plastic square.

"But the drone," Mom whined.

Gary freed the machine from the net. Its blades whirled. He tossed it in the air, and it flew away. "Article 9, subsection B, no property of the HOA can be *destroyed*. It's fine."

"You read that thing?" Dad asked. "I can't get through the brochure."

"Know your enemy," Gary snarled, making his way back towards the house.

The sound of metal crunching came from the front yard. A truck revved hard, spinning its tires. We got to the front window just in time to see Gary's creation bending forwards. A two-inch chain wrapped around its midsection extended into the street. Rebar moaned, straining against the concrete as a tow truck built to haul eighteen-wheelers pulled against the dormant creature.

"It'll never hold," I said, shaking my head at my brother.

"It doesn't have to," Gary said, grinning at me like he just pinched the Mona Lisa. "It's not supposed to."

Half the crane/heron/flamingo tore away. The car door wings flew across the grass, cutting a gash in our lawn, leaving nothing but the rebar legs and what was, I suppose, the groin.

I narrowed my eyes at Gary. "You were just trying to piss her off."

"Article 6, Section 12, destruction of an art installation. Article 9, section 4, operation of industrial vehicle. Article 4, section 23, tilling soil to make a garden," Gary rattled off.

Mom gleamed her peroxide smile. "That's enough to get her banned from the HOA."

Dad put a hand on Gary's shoulder and squeezed a proud squeeze. "Hell, that might even be enough to have her banished from the street."

I glanced over at my brother. "You know, they haven't said anything about lime-green flamingos."

Gary cocked his head. "If we make them look more like dodos, they could go under Article 50, Section 5274, because they're extinct."

I nodded. "If we make them light up, could they be considered safety lights?"

"Way ahead of you," he said, heading for his room. "If I use wood stakes for legs, we might classify them as tree supports."

"You're an evil one," I said to Gary.

"Yeah, well, birds of a feather . . ."

Foreverland

A. W. McCollough

The fucking waiter was also a flamingo. Curved bill dipping politely, they pulled a sheaf of menus from under their wing with one foot, balancing on the other. "My name is Flannery, I'll be your flamingo today. Would you care for a menu? We have freshly-printed Flamingo Burgers on special, Jimmy Cricket Croquets, (crickets are raised right here at Foreverland in the greenhouse), and a Sea Jelly Waldorf."

The entire cafe, far as I could see, filled with the neuro-augmented pink dodgers, dipping and bobbing, stalking smoothly through the crowded tables and tiki torches, carrying wide trays on their backs. Our flamingo fanned the sheaf of menus and paused, expectantly. I shrugged, set my breath mask on the table, and hung my cane over the back of the empty chair next to me. My damn hip tweaked as I sat, and Eugene was there instantly catching my elbow and helping me down. Goddamn, I used to leave him puffing in my dust. Too damn old.

Our flamingo, not receiving an answer, pivoted and bobbed neatly on their standing leg, snapping out each menu from between their pink-webbed foot like thrown cards that landed, like some preposterous trick beside our water glasses. "If you have no questions? I'll give you some time to decide?"

"Eugene, why ever would you bring me here on Walt Day?" Eugene looked at his menu, not answering the question. Answering questions had never been his forte. I'd always hated the Mouse and everything it stood for, but he'd nonetheless brought me to the end of all theme parks on the one day a year I would hate it the most. Fucking Walt Fucking Day.

"You know my work is important, Justin," Eugene said.

"You really couldn't get a different day off?" Come to think of it, it would have been a miracle if he had. He'd never taken a day off for family before.

Eugene shook his head and held up his menu to Flannery, our flamingo waiter. "This Full English Dodo, how is it?" Eugene tapped lamination half as thick as his own fingernails. Nails had come back in, apparently. I could hardly keep up with the virals these days, nor cared to. I hadn't done my nails since before Florida blew into the Gulf.

"Dodo sausage, eggs, and black pudding. Cricket meal toast (crickets are raised right here in our greenhouse) and baked soybeans. We receive many compliments."

"Never had it yourself then?" I asked. Fancy a waiter not eating the food. Red flag, I say.

"I mainly subsist on small invertebrates or cyanobacteria, myself, so can't say that I have." Flannery dipped gracefully on their standing leg, the neural augmenter wrapped around their head flashed a jeweled line of lights between their feathers. "But we make a mean Lake Natron Smoothie here to die for. A feast of nutritious red or green algae in a salty, high pH slurry. I can recommend."

"Sounds tasty, what do you think, Justin?" Eugene, casting a glance at me.

"It is, but I would have to see your Exit card before I could serve you, unfortunately. Or certificate of durable gene edits for extremophile environments." Flannery paused, tilting their crooked beak to one side. "No?"

"I'm looking forward to the rollercoaster, Eugene. I'm in no hurry, I'll pass on the red tide slushy."

Eugene snapped his menu closed. "The Full English Dodo for me, then. And you'll have the Sea Jelly Waldorf."

"I'm quite old enough to order for myself, thank you. Too old." I glanced down at the blurry menu in front of me, then back up to Flannery. "Yes, the Waldorf, please." Eugene knew me, all too well, after all.

Flannery flamingo switched legs. "Box, Moon, Nomura's, or Irukandji?"

"Irukandji?"

"Ah, I'll have to see your Exit card for that or the Box, I'm afraid. Cardiac arrest and what not. Quite painful, I believe, if that is what you are wanting." Our flamingo seemed appropriately abashed at having mentioned Exit twice in a conversation, their eyes blinked rapidly.

"Nomura's then, thank you."

Flamingo Flannery danced away between the shifting bustle of other flamingos. Now that I had noticed them, I saw them throughout the park. Thousands of them, collecting trash, running the rides, driving small golf carts along the concrete paths, leading groups of tourists. Eugene followed my gaze and sat forward.

"There must be a story there, Justin, I'll ask Flannery when they come back with the food."

"Please don't. I'm sure it would be embarrassing."

"No trouble at all. Speaking of trouble," Eugene ran a hand through his black hair, "Did you get through the paperwork ok? I can send over my lawyer, if that would be easier."

Now that I'd made the decision, he seemed more helpful than ever. Hah. But he did have great hair. Would always have great hair, come to that, after the treatments.

"I'm decrepit, lame, thirty years behind the fashion trends, and losing my hair, but I can still sign my name." I took an angry sip of water in my dry mouth, swallowed carefully around the lump in my throat.

"No one signs their name anymore, Justin. That's what DNA is for. I'm more concerned with the details, making sure this is what you want. You can always change your mind."

"Sound mind I have, and have had, for time and long enough. I've always been stubborn."

"True, Debbie could never convince you to eat carrots." Eugene sat back in his chair, crossed his legs easily, and laughed. "You would sit at the table for hours."

"Disgusting things. I'm glad they no longer exist." My mouth felt full of orange mush, and I sipped at my water. "She always overcooked them."

Eugene frowned, "Debbie did her best. I won't have you talking bad about your mother."

Twenty years after the divorce and he still got tense when she came up. "Never her, just her cooking. You have to admit, Eugene, that wasn't her forte. Wednesday night pork chops?

You would sneak takeout from Andy's past her to the garage, after dinner. We'd play video games and eat burgers."

"Benji got fat on those pork chops." Eugene relaxed and sat back. "Loved that dog. Should have had him cloned, really."

I shuddered but ignored the remark. No need to spoil a last theme park trip over an argument that we'd been around more times than a traffic circle. He never could let things go, while I dropped them too easily. But really, the treatments were just plastic all over again. I had no desire to join the mounds of indigestible humans clogging the planet. Recycling starts at home.

I cleared my throat, "Whatever happened to Andy's? I'd kill for another Double Cheese Double Burger." Two fat beef patties held together by their mutual love of melted cheddar, pickled jalapeños sliced flavor thin, and Andy's Awesome Burger Sauce bringing it all home. Damn. The thought of the Sea Jelly Waldorf in my immediate future filled me with despair.

"Here we are," Flannery swooped back, gliding as if on ice, one foot reaching up like a pink feathered Yoga instructor to balance an oval tray on their splayed foot. "The Full English Dodo and a Sea Jelly Waldorf." Flannery seamlessly juggled tray, table, and plates until each plate alighted correctly. They held up a grinder, "May I offer smoked cricket dust? No? Enjoy!" Flannery bobbled, then turned to go.

"Oh, Flannery!"

"Yes? Would you care for the cricket dust after all?" Flannery completed two eager twists of the grinder before Eugene waved them away.

"Please don't, Eugene." He was intent on embarrassing me.

"No, no. I was just wondering, there are so many of your people here. Why is that? When did you migrate?" Eugene punctuated his sentence with a bite of Dodo sausage, grunting his approval as he did.

I bowed my head over the Sea Jelly Waldorf, pretending not to listen, and forked up a strip of bias-cut jellyfish covered in mayonnaise. Crunchy, a mild salt flavor nearly lost in the mayo. An odd grit of walnut, whose bitterness, I decided, didn't work. Overall, not bad. Not an Andy's DCDB, but I wouldn't have fed it to Benji.

Flannery bobbed, cleared their throat, and said, "We've always been here, off and on, ranging from the far south up to Florida. Between our traditional breeding lakes drained for rare earths, hotter years, and declining food stocks, my flamboyance flew up to the Keyes. After the Great Blow hit the state, those of us that survived came out west. We're pretty well adapted to wading in toxic waters, so most of us, once we got our augments, took up clearing waste ponds in the valley. But Foreverland had some openings, so, beats wading in sludge all day."

"I imagine so. Justin, did you hear that? Fascinating. And the augments? On credit, I suppose?"

"Some of us were the first through the Berkeley Augment program. Those early birds sponsored the rest of us, but—"

"Eugene, please. Leave the poor bird in peace and eat your breakfast for lunch." I nodded to Flannery. "Thank you."

They hesitated for a moment, then bobbled and glided away.

Lunch was awkward for a while, but then our conversation drifted back to comfortable topics. Friends that had had the treatment. Eugene's plans to go on a round-the-world tour, once he could get the time off work. He never would, I knew. Eugene had spent the night I was born finishing the quarterly reports. It shocked me that he'd made it today.

Turned out that not even printed beef could keep Andy's in business, once the culture had shifted toward veg, and besides, printed was never the same. They'd turned it into a treatment center, turns out. I hope they got a good price on the building, at least.

The afternoon wore down to evening and the conversation to silence. "It's time," I said, reaching for my cane and breath mask. I looked around for Flannery, but couldn't pick him out of the rest of the flamboyance bustling among the tables. I left an extra ten percent for Eugene's intrusiveness, and we left.

The walk through Foreverland was quiet, but pleasant. Flamingos everywhere, of course, but now I knew why and where they came from. That was something, I suppose, to thank Eugene for.

Ahead, Urbonas Maximus towered over Foreverland, a tall curve and seven silvery curlicues written across the sky like the steel signature of a giant. The original design was the gift of a morbid genius of an artist last century. A few seconds of free-fall from the peak, then into those ten-G clothoid spirals, grey fading swiftly to black. My step picked up, just a bit.

I'd reached the gate when Eugene grabbed my arm. He'd never been good at silence, or saying anything important until it was too late. Well, almost too late.

"I blame myself, son. Justin." Eugene's face resembled wet newspaper in a pile. He sniffled behind his breath mask.

"Don't. Don't carry that away from today. You did okay, Dad. Really. You couldn't have done better. This is my path, I chose it. I just can't anymore, don't want to. It's nothing you did."

Breath masks were not designed for wiping eyes, his tears followed the cut of his mask around his nose and mouth, collecting in tremulous drops on the silicone chin piece, the bubbles along one edge indicated a weak seal. "Get your mask fit-checked, would you? You always forget. That's going get you killed some day."

"Not likely," Eugene choked, "I got all the upgrades."

And that was all either of us had to say. I left him and his wet eyes by the gate with the sign reading, "You must be this old to ride this ride" next to a picture of Santa Claus, and climbed into the first car of Urbonas Maximus. My cane slotted neatly into the provided holder, locking in place.

I shifted uncomfortably on the hard plastic seat, sighed.

Finally.

Months deciding, then endless arguments, suffering well-intended suggestions, paperwork and more paperwork, for more months. All done.

A wind-chime sounded, soothing, signaling the start of the Urbonas. An uneasy murmur rose behind me, some of the other riders were perhaps more thrill seekers than serious. They said some people took two or three rides, half-way, before committing. I'm more of the "measure twice cut once" type, myself.

The coaster took twenty minutes to climb to the peak five hundred meters above Foreverland. Plenty of time if anyone wanted to hit the panic button. It would pause there, at the peak, a legally mandated ten minutes for any last-minute defectors.

Which there were. A good dozen took a silvery elevator back down to dirt and whatever tangle of lives they still had.

I was not one of them. I'd planned this for years, since it became legal with the passage of the Graceful Exit laws. This was my right, my choice. I savored the last view of my city, the sun setting into a sea that had crept ever closer over the years. I took a long breath through my mask, then glanced at the AQI reading in the HUD. Under three hundred today, hell, my lungs could take that without burning. I pulled of my mask and sucked on the raw stuff. It tasted like diesel, wildfire, and dust. Like childhood.

I walked my eyes along the distant cliff edge coast, back along the low foothills rising above the bay. Somewhere along there, just this side of the monorail, Eugene still lived in the same house. Upgraded, of course, just like him, but he'd kept my room, built the extension around the treehouse in back rather than cutting the oak down. He never could let anything go.

A flamboyance of flamingos, their pink black against the sunset, rose from the fence line east of Foreverland and sailed seaward. The chime sounded again, and I flew with them.

The Contendings
Lara Messersmith-Glavin

It gets awesome dark in the Valley at night. When the black-outs take the shine, ain't nothing left to spark your way but what sludge glows green at the bottom of the Nilla as it bunches and slides through the Valley like a great, fat snake. It's the only river left in these parts, flooding and draining, thick and dark, stinking as it goes, splitting the neighbor-hoods like a watery knife—Kings, Memphis, Ramesside. Each slice of the Valley is its own turf with its own crew to run it. Us, we're the N.E.A.D.[1], and Ramesside is ours.

Civ here is dense—concrete canyons, all motos and markets. We all tucked into our dens like termites. We got warehouses pushed right up on the riverbank, so we don't got to move things far afoot. The Valley nights may be dark, but daytime Amun is so hot and bright, it shines down crazy mad. Hard to be stealth when it's up top. So we stay close to Nilla, cuz

---

1   Near East Autonomous Distribution network

Nilla moves it all: skin slaves, wet tech, talk-boxes, all manner of ups and downs, glory bobs and sorrow bits. Smugglers pushing their little boats packed with nasties and wants. Our crew tells it how to move, so we got the power. Ain't no power in Ramesside but what come with the fist and the flow, hear me? That's why when that new crew moved in and Falco found the old boss, O'Shearus, all cut up into little bits around the Valley, we knew things were about to get real hurt.

The new crew call themselves The Set, and their boss swagger round like he shits amber. Cousin Faiyum say he looks like a bird[2], but first time I lay my eyes on him, I think, "He an animal." Jackal, he calls himself, and I think he's right.

He come strutting into our place one day, all sharp-faced and showing skin, all flash and chipped up, swinging heat and acting like he gonna take Falco's seat. We all know Falco gonna take over N.E.A.D. now O'Shearus is dead. O'Shea been like a father to Falco, and so no dog-looking flamingo-faced sisterfucker gonna sit his ass on what throne go rightful to him. Jackal though, he's thinking no snot-nose kid should be having such access, hear me? He and his crew, they from outside, they seen things, they know what's what

---

2   In *The Book of the Faiyum*, a "topographical priestly manual" for the crocodile god Sobek (dating as far back as 332 BCE), Set is pictured as having the head of a flamingo in his conflict with Horus. Other accounts describe him as resembling, variously, a jackal, donkey, giraffe, fennec fox, okapi, or aardvark.

in the Valley and even *out there* . . . out where nobody go. They *Wasteland* folk, for true, even with all that bling round his neck. He says that make him the right choice to hold the flow in Ramesside.

'Course we all thinking, "Oh! Damn."
And, "Shut the fuck up—I wanna see this."

Trial 1: Hippopotami

It was Falco who swung first. Course maybe that was not so smart, cuz next thing we know, Jackal ducked under that big old scythe of a punch and *boom!* He pushes his head straight into Falco's gut and *splash!* They both go right off the ledge into the river.

We near the Nilla, night and Amun-time, but that don't mean I want to drink it. Whatever still can live in the bruise of that river ain't a friend of mine, and nothing that glow gonna go in this mouth, hear? But there they went, Jackal and Falco, all tangled up like asps in a basket. Falco is strong but I don't know if he can swim, not that the two of them were doing much swimming. More like Jackal be holding him under, like they seeing who can hold their breath the longest down there in that stinking dark. Falco not even thrashing or splash-ing—like he so stubborn he gonna wait it out down there with that Wastelander freak, just to show him who's boss. No bubbles coming up. No nothing, just sludge and shadow.

Then Isa pushed through the crowd, right, cuz we all standing around watching this thing like a thick of sheep. But she
was O'Shea's girl, queen-like, got no patience for this kind
of dick-swinging, and she pulls out her heat just like that
and aims the laser right into the Nilla, where the murk and
the funk aswirl. She took one straight shot at Jackal, like
she gonna end this business once and for all. But you know
what—that water do some crazy bend to that light, and zap!
she laze his ass, but don't you know it go *zap-zap!* and she laze
Falco, too. The green murk cooked brown with the blood of
them both, and Isa she screaming, and we all just stand there,
like, what the fuck now. They both dead.

Then a hand reaches up out the water, and before you know
it, Falco and Jackal, not dead even a little, they're pulling
themselves out onto the ledge, the concrete ramp slick with
muck cuz the river low. These asps fighting now for real, both
all soaking wet and full of reek, slime and shit streaking their
faces, their hair, their bling. Falco got this grimace like he
wants to eat the Jackal's heart between the punches. Jackal
all snarl and snap, we can't tell what's an elbow and what's a
knee, you hear me? That creature sharp. They both rolling
around and we all afraid to get involved. I'm looking at my
crew and they just shaking their heads like, "This ain't yours,
cousin. You let it be." So I let it be.

Next thing I know, Jackal retching into the muck. Falco done
got him in the balls, maybe busted one off for all I know. Jackal's eyes look like they gonna pop right out of his head. That

big bare chest and those blings all swinging, now he gone pale and soft. He shaking on the wet cement. I think this is it, he's done for, and Falco does too, cuz he turns and gets up smiling, nodding to his crew like he knew it, when Jackal lunges up and grabs his face from behind. It happened so fast, I don't know what I'm seeing until Jackal hold up something, this big old dog-shit grin on his face, blood smearing across his cheeks and down his fingers and wrist. Falco is making sounds like someone just ripped out his eyeball, and you know, that's what that sisterfucker just did.

Isa shrieks. She sobbing, like it's all her fault that she didn't shoot that Wastelander in the head when she had the chance. Falco got one hand plastered over the bloody wreck in his face, gore leaking down between his fingers and into the collar of his shirt. He dripping, muck and water and blood, leaving nasty footprints as he stomps right up to Isa and smacks her across the face, awesome loud. The N.E.A.D all take a step back as one, eyeing the wet print glowing across her cheek, as she falls on her ass. All but T-hoth, that saintly fuck, who steps toward her and offers his hand, pulls her up.

"Stupid cow," he hisses.

Trial 2: Lettuce

Now this next bit, of course, I didn't see. I mean, our crew is tight and all, but we don't roll like *that*.

But what I hear was that later that night, I guess Jackal got horny from having his nutsack ripped off, cuz he made his way into Falco's room, all stealth. I guess Wastelanders just built different. Jackal takes off his shirt to show his big skin and the bling that makes him a man with fists, you hear? And I don't know, maybe Falco was thinking what he saw wasn't all that bad. Jackal, he starts making like maybe the two of them could share a seat, like they'd be real good together. He's talking power this and flow that, his lying lips all hot against Falco's ears. His talking hands all soft strokes here and there. He's got him spooned up, maybe—those hard muscles warm and dry, not stinking so much now. Little resin makes him smell fine. Maybe he's all oil-slick, little glint here in the dark where there ain't much shine. He got his big hands saying hello to Falco's dick, which says hello back, and then he turns that boss over and goes to make him his bitch.

So Jackal, he's all hard as a stick, and he's thinking he's gonna plow this ass like a field. But Falco's not stupid, he knows he can't just bottom up for the man who cut his daddy up into little pieces, so he reaches down and makes himself a pussy from his hands, and after all the grunting and sweating, he catches that big Wastelander load and tells Jackal to get the fuck out, go back to his own digs to sleep. I guess Falco ain't no cuddler.

Then Falco go straight to Isa and tells her that Jackal tried to fuck him up the ass. Now, you ask me, this ain't boss-like behavior, but who am I to talk? No boss, that's for true. Then

Isa, she gets all pissed off and smacks his hands—she's still burnt up from when he mad earlier—and makes him wash up real good, scrubs his dirty claws till they're raw and red. She wants nothing to do with that Jackal jizz. She knows he's only tattling on old dog-boy flamingo-face cuz he still kinda hot for him, his dick still awake and looking around for the party, so she dunks her hands in some sani-goo and jerks his junk right then and there, grabs that load for herself and puts it in a little jar. For true, now.

The next morning, that woman shows she's used to dealing with boss bullshit, cuz she goes to the kitchen and makes one awesome snack, takes that little jar and smears Falco's cum right across the flatbread and layers up all meats and veg and such. And then she marches straight through the concrete canyons along the river and finds the den where Jackal and his Set been hanging out, and she offers that fiend a sandwich like some kind of peace offering.

Jackal, now, is sprawled out in his den, thinking he's the biggest dog in the pile. He's got a freshly pumped dick, and here's the lady of the house come to bring him a snack, so he wolfs that thing down without a thought to pain or poison. Ask me, it's none too smart. He gets so swagger, he thinks now is the time for him to stroll back into Ramesside and kick Falco off the seat for good.

When he shows up—and this part I saw—we're all there, all making busy in our hideout along the Nilla. Some boys smoking, some soaking up some Amun rays, some counting out the last shipment of hot wet tech. Jackal's chest is puffed out, his bling shining something awesome, and he stands like it's time for a speech from the pharoah.

"You all want a bitch for a king?" he shouts. "Cuz that what you getting: a little bitch-king who takes it up the canal."

The N.E.A.D. crew snickers and shifts, like, shit is awkward, right? But then Isa steps up, wearing her mom-face, and we all go quiet.

"Falco ain't got a lick of jizz on him, dog. You the one been sucking cum."

Gasps. Titters.

Jackal's face turns red like he spent all day baking in Amun, but T-hoth stands up, those weird eyes of his weirding. I said before only power in Ramesside is fist and flow, but that ain't quite right. T-hoth got some other power that no one else got, something can't be sold or bought or threatened. He knows things, feels things, sees things in that silver stare that we got no business knowing. Gives me the shivers.

Now that creepy fuck comes toward the two bosses and holds out his hands, like he got some magical cum-detector or something, and it's crazy cuz Isa's right—Falco is clean. He done got scrubbed free of that Jackal jizz. But *Jackal*—T-hoth runs his hands over that puffed up chest, through the bling and the shine, and when he gets to the belly he stops. For true, his eyes go all bright and he can tell that Jackal been eating that cum sandwich, can feel that load sitting there in his guts. He keeps his hands there, like he gonna show us all, and we're thinking, "Fuck no, you don't gotta show us." But he does. And you think that cum gonna just come back out the Jackal's mouth? Not a little. It starts pouring out his ears, like Falco done shot pure light, running up that dog-looking head like gravity flipped to the sky. Jackal's scared now, cuz he knows something's up, and Isa got that smile that say he's right. But T-hoth just keep doing his weird cum magic, till all that Falco-foam run up Jackal's head and make a big circle.

Like a disc. Like a gem.

T-hoth reached up and plucked that crazy cum-circle off Jackal's head and put it on his hat like he been waiting for it all along.

Trial 3: Stone boats

All of us in N.E.A.D. were pretty much set that Falco had proved himself fit for the seat at this point, but Jackal wouldn't let it rest. He was thinking that if he couldn't win with fists, maybe he could win with flow. So back to the Nilla we all went.

Those two were gonna race smuggler's boats through the Ramesside canals, and whoever gets to the end first keeps the terrain and the crews. But Falco, he was ready. He filled the bottom of Jackal's boat with cement, so when the two took off, Jackal's feet sunk down all heavy like baby flamingoes on the salt flats, the ones what get eat by hyenas.

The N.E.A.D. laugh like a pack of those hyenas, pointing and jerking at the look on Jackal's face as his boat wobbled under the weight. Falco give him a little wave and set off down the canal into the first tunnel, motor whirring, but Jackal stuck in place, drifting in the toxic current, can't move the boat faster or move his body at all. The cement heavy, and soon, thick slops of Nilla lap their way over the sides like hungry tongues. The filth and the murk pool in the bottom of the boat as it hangs lower in the water, then lower. Jackal howls and curses as the Nilla swallow him up and take his body down, the thick stink of it filling his sharp-toothed mouth until it go quiet. And then the boat was gone, eat up by the river and all its filthy secrets.

We cheered and there was a big big party that night for Falco when he claimed the seat that once belonged to O'Shearus. And though it was dark, T-hoth's hat glowed brightly as the moon, bringing awesome shine to Ramesside.

Flood

Cody T Luff

The streets of the city were still, four inches of floodwater reflecting sky over the blacktop, Chuck's van gliding through, cutting a ripple that shattered against the bellies of parked cars and front stoops. Fourth big storm that season, another record breaker. Chuck eased the van past an abandoned firetruck, dark windshield staring as he went by. He couldn't blame folks for living out here, property behind the flood wall was beyond the reach of most. He was lucky in that aspect. His parents' house just happened to be two blocks in from the gate. He'd never made enough to move out and that proved to be a stroke of luck. Maybe his only stroke.

Service calls to Placid were always complicated. When the company ran high-density cable out here, they were cavalier concerning the residents' access to uninterrupted power even before the flood wall went up. Now, just a few years on, most residents of Placid made do with a mix of budget solar and what was still coming out of the city. You paid your due or you made do out in Placid.

High-density cable repair wasn't his calling but it, amongst several other pick-up jobs, kept Chuck on his side of the flood wall. It wasn't hard if you didn't count the service calls to Placid. It ate time and spit out money so that was good enough. For now.

Chuck's GPS display flickered across the windshield, reminding him to turn right at the intersection with a pulsing yellow arrow. The intersection in question was cut in half by a downed tree. He slowed the van and chewed on his lip. Three kids sat on the buckled trunk, plastic rain boots dangling like colorful fruit. One waved at Chuck, muddy face housing a grin that didn't belong in Placid. Chuck tapped the horn, waved and pulled the van onto the sidewalk, skirting the tree. He was already two hours late.

The Commons at Riverside squatted in the flood water. A stack of apartments with small squinting windows. Portable solar panels studded the flat rooftop, dull metallic wings of imagined square birds. A Water Safety crew worked out front, lights flashing on their pickup trucks. They paid no attention as Chuck parked, slipped free of his van and splashed his way into the Commons courtyard. A few people stood leaning on the rails of the upper levels, smoking and staring into their phones. Two more kids were floating an old basketball back and forth in the courtyard, jeans hiked up to their thighs, shivering. Chuck frowned, splashed his way to the stairs and climbed. Apartment 188, double platinum subscription, unlimited data plan. The door opened before he could knock.

"You're really late," 188 said, waving Chuck inside.

Two steps in and Chuck knew 188 was a body jock. Data cable stapled to the walls of the little entryway, thick as a firehose, a snake slick in its black plastic skin. The heat alone would have been a good clue but the Interface in the living room was the final piece of evidence.

"I apologize, I'm afraid the flood . . ." Chuck rummaged in his work kit for the plastic booties he wore over his shoes during a service call.

"Yeah, that's fine, I just need to be up and running as soon as possible, okay?" 188 was tall, black hair pulled up into a frizzing knot, a floppy set of ugly brown pajamas wrapped in an uglier bathrobe the color of spilled wine. "You don't need those, the floors are already filthy."

Which, Chuck thought, wasn't true. The apartment was small, an open square with a corner kitchen, a daybed piled with an old quilt, a sagging bookshelf made of cinderblocks and salvaged 2x4s, and 188's Interface. A beautiful padded recliner with chrome skull plugs dangling from the ceiling-mount like dentist equipment. Generation 3, damn near an antique but Chuck could already see the love that went into its care.

"I'm sorry, I have to wear them to avoid accidental static discharge when working on your data cables." He tried out a smile on 188, she didn't smile back. "I'll be in and out as fast as I can, I promise."

188 crossed her arms and frowned, the belt of her robe dangling near a bare ankle. "Thanks."

Chuck caught a flash of movement. A black cat blinked at him before oozing under the daybed. "Whoa! You have a cat? I've been trying to get a license for a year . . ." He caught himself and grimaced.

"I don't have a license. Outside the flood wall," 188 said.

"Ah, uh, yeah. I better take a look at your service unit."

The box was located in one of the two kitchen cabinets.

Chuck set up a work light and keyed the faceplate open. "So . . . that's a great Interface, by the way."

188 leaned on the little kitchen stove, her eyes on Chuck. "It's old."

"Gen 3. When they still came with chrome as a standard option. I have a Gen 6 at home." Chuck started a diagnostic and watched numbers tick on his handheld before glancing back at 188. "Gen 3 was before they added the sensory inhibitors."

188's expression melted away into stone. "That's right."

"I bet it's a killer rig. I do a little body jocking on the side. I signed with MagnaFit, you know the autogym? I mostly pilot on gym equipment but I just got a Pilates certification, so I'll have that as an option." The data scroll on his handheld stopped. "Whoa, you're rolling 120 plus petabytes?"

"That's the problem. I need 300." 188's frown was back.

"No worries, we'll get you back up to speed," Chuck pulled fresh cable from his work kit and glanced at 188's Interface. "Yeah, Gen 3 is perfect for that load. Really is something. I love to see equipment like that in the wild."

"What's an autogym?" 188 shuffled behind him, the little refrigerator opened.

"You don't know about those? Pretty neat. Subscribers hire a body jock to pilot a workout while they game or, you know, just bliss out in the consciousness buffer. I have a handful of clients, my favorite is a big-time gamer. He is 'scribed for two-hour workouts four times a week. I plug in, pilot him to the autogym, drag his body through two hours of elliptical and pilot him back. He gets to game in the buffer, doesn't feel a thing." Chuck stopped working, pointed his screwdriver at 188's Interface. "Neither of us does, Gen 6 edits out the fatigue while I'm piloting. He only gets the hangover. You're Gen 3, you'd end up with the full experience."

"I'm not a body jock." 188 dropped two cups onto the counter, the smell of instant coffee rich in the little kitchen.

"That for me? Thank you." Chuck drained the cup in one gulp and raised the empty cup with a smile. "I needed that."

"I remember reading about something like that," 188 said. "The autogym."

Chuck pulled old cable from the service unit with a grunt. He dropped it on the worn tile floor and nodded. "There was a bit of an uproar a few years ago. Some big-league athletes set up one of the first autogyms. Fans weren't really happy. I mean, it worked out. Do you remember Bradley Durst?"

188 shook her head no and sipped her coffee.

"He was making appearances in the buffer, doing interviews and running an avatar around the net while a body jock piloted his training. Die-hard fans were pissed. They wanted Bradley to do his own stunts, so to speak, but the training was good and his season was better. Dear old Bradley tripled his payday by being everywhere at once. Worked out for everyone."

"How does anyone know if Bradley isn't being . . . piloted when he's playing . . . what does he play?" 188 set her cup down.

"Ah," Chuck leaned into the question, a smile growing, "that's the thing, right? Basketball, by the way. Killer power forward. Now the league is requiring data-traffic monitoring for players. Not too serious yet but as the Interface gets better, they'll need to sniff harder. I should be out of your way in twenty minutes or so."

188 watched him work. Chuck was used to it. He wouldn't trust a tech to go mucking about in his data setup either. He stole glances of the Gen 3 while he worked. The seat was custom, black breathable mesh padding resting on a graceful metal curve. The skull plugs were bright, clean cables gathered in a smart cinch. An old flat-screen display was mounted to the left arm rest, wood-paneled inlay giving the set up a touch of the organic. A puffy flamingo sticker graced the head cushion. Long and red, a graceful neck curling to a stylized face. You could tell a lot about a body jock by the state of their Interface.

"You said you're not a jock," Chuck queued another diagnostic and wiped his forehead.

"I'm not," 188 answered.

"So, what are you doing with an Interface. A Gen 3, no less."

188 frowned and draw her robe more tightly closed.

"Hey, I'm sorry. I'm just a geek. Your Interface got me curious, I . . ."

"I'm a Trauma Proxy."

Chuck blinked. He turned to 188, his handheld forgotten. That explained 188's data usage.

"Do you know what that is?" 188's eyes found his.

"Yeah. You're a death doula."

188 shook her head and stepped away from the kitchen. "No, doula is the wrong word. The media screwed that one up. Proxy is better."

Chuck set his handheld down and followed 188 to the living room. She stood by her Interface, one hand on an armrest. "What do you mean?"

"It's like your autogym. Except I don't pilot anyone anywhere. I . . . go along with them. Help them out when it gets too much. Maybe copilot is the way to think about it."

Chuck stood for a moment. He'd heard about trauma proxies before. They were around before full piloting was developed. He'd never met one in person but both 188's data usage and her Interface made sense now.

"That's why you been burning data. You get the full sensory map of your . . . uh . . . clients, right? You feel the works."

188 shook her head no again. "I share it."

"Share it?"

188 leaned against the armrest. "Think of it like piloting your workouts but instead of editing out the muscle fatigue, you and your client share the load."

Chuck's handheld beeped in the kitchen. He started to turn before glancing back at 188. "You share . . . death?"

"Almost finished?" 188 gestured with her chin.

Chuck blinked and smiled. "You bet, I'll just finish up real quick." Chuck finished his installation, testing data speeds before closing the unit and gathering his tools and the old cables from the floor. He'd spent a month looking at body jock options available on the net before he'd settled on getting the necessary implants and picking up his Gen 6 Interface from an online dealership. He'd spent the following month doing simple body-jocking. Going to the dentist for a guy in New York, running shopping errands for a woman in Denver, even walking dogs as a subcontractor for a college student out in Jersey. It paid well enough, and the Interface handled most of the mobility and dexterity issues, so Chuck had simply been executive function for hire. The autogym was the first gig that paid enough to justify his expenses and his recent foray into jocking for leveling-up gamers in the consciousness buffer while they were at work was starting to pay out. But being an Interface death doula? That was beyond his imagining.

"Okay, you are up and running." Chuck stood with his gear dangling from his shoulders.

188 was already in her Interface, skull plugs in hand. "Thanks. Sorry if I was a little . . . brusque at first. I have a client I need to get back to."

"That's understandable, no worries." Chuck smiled and glanced at the flamingo sticker on 188's head cushion. "I like that. Nice touch."

188 followed his gaze and smiled. "That was a joke. I have a nurse come by during my long stints. I need an IV if I am in for longer than ten hours."

"Ten hours? That's a long haul . . ."

188 nodded. "The longest I've managed is a week."

Chuck blinked in surprise.

"My nurse, Kimmie, she stuck that to my Interface after that. She said I look like a flamingo when I'm working. I think it's the curve of the chair, you know? And maybe the skull plugs pull my head down, I'm not sure. But after a while it just seemed to fit. We started calling ourselves flamingos."

"You and your nurse?"

"Yes. And the group of proxies I advertise with." 188 ran a fingertip over the sticker, a smile flickering. "They're beautiful birds. Were beautiful birds. I sometimes forget they went extinct."

Chuck glanced away as if he was watching something deeply private.

"They did everything together, you know? Stood together in that way, curving together. So it stuck."

"Pardon the pun," Chuck said.

"Pardon the pun," 188 smiled.

"Can I ask you something?" Chuck pulled up his belt, his head at an angle.

188's smile faded, but she nodded yes.

"Is it . . . worth it? The pain? I mean, does it pay well?"

188 stared at him for a long moment, skull plugs still in hand. "Sometimes the pay is good. Depends on who's dying."

"That came out wrong, I'm sorry . . . "

188 leaned forward in the Interface, her fingers bringing the flat screen to life. "No, I understand what you meant. About half of my clients can't pay. Part of my job is finding ways to get them the implants necessary for the Interface and money for the service. People die every day, what I do is not exactly what you do. I help them get there, take on some of what they feel. But mostly I'm there with them. Inside."

"You walk them to the door," Chuck said.

188 offered a small smile. "Exactly."

"Have you ever . . . walked through . . . with them?"

188's expression remained unchanged. "Thank you for the work. I should get back to my client."

"Of course. Just call again if you need me . . . uh, I mean the company, the service, just call again . . . "

The city remained drowned outside. Rain clouds hunched overhead, their black and blue bellies heavy. Chuck deposited his gear and slid into the driver's seat of his van. He had two more calls in Placid, time marched on. But he stayed where he was, his eyes following a lone woman wading down the middle of the street, bags of groceries held out in front of her, halting step by halting step. After a moment, he stepped back into the street, waving one hand at the woman, his voice offering to help her get where she was going as ripples raced away from his reflection.

When

Kate Ristau

When the flamingo appeared, I thought I was going to die.

It started as a joke. Jane told me she had finally planted the garden. I rolled my eyes and followed her outside. The garden bed was empty, except for one lone pink flamingo.

"Kia, isn't it gorgeous?" she said.

I stared at its Pepto Bismol feathers.

"Absolutely smashing, darling."

We were so droll back then. Careful British accents and feigned indifference. Trained by years in Idaho spent chasing polite society on Downton Abbey.

But when the flamingo showed up in the shower, I smiled.

"She's a dirty bird," Jane said, and I laughed outright.

Then I took an Instagram photo.

Everyone thinks that the best moments of your life are like your wedding, or the birth of your kid. I'm sure those are super great. But we never had any kids, and our church wouldn't let us get married back then, so I never had a yardstick to measure things right.

I just know that birthdays are stupid, holidays are trash, and that plastic pink flamingo made little moments better.

Like when my cousin ruined Thanksgiving. Jane and I sat out on the cold back step after he peeled out of the driveway and left me with all those nasty, whispered words. Sweet potato pie on the counter and I couldn't imagine eating it. Bullshit. Fucking bullshit. People shouldn't mess with pie.

Jane got up and grabbed the flamingo and stuck it in the flower pot next to me.

"We shouldn't invite him again," she said.

"We shouldn't invite *any* of them again."

She looked out at the backyard, then at the flamingo, then back at me. "Okay."

"Okay," I said.

And we went back inside holding hands.

We ate the pie, we said goodbye, and the next year, we had our own Thanksgiving. With Tofurkey and homemade cranberry sauce and five different types of pie.

The flamingo was the centerpiece.

Jane was always doing shit like that. Centerpieces. Place cards. Tiny folded napkins. It was beautiful and maddening and made things complicated and perfect.

Things were great until they weren't, and I don't want to talk about that. I don't. No. It's all bullshit without the pie.

I can hear her in my head: write it down. Write it down. Start with WHEN.

Fine. When.

When she got diagnosed, she introduced me to her therapist.
When I said no, she gave me a notebook.
When I didn't write in it, she put my phone inside it.
When she got her labs back, she cried.
When she started coughing, I couldn't breathe.
When she woke up from surgery, I was holding her hand.
When she died, so did I.

When
When
When
When

Nothing came after. Nothing. No words. No spaces. No letters. Just me. Sitting on the back step. By myself. Without her. How? Head in my hands. Tired. Always so tired. Why? I couldn't sleep. No. I couldn't be awake. No. I couldn't without her.

I wouldn't without her.

I didn't.

The first day the flamingo moved, I thought I was dreaming. I blinked and it was gone.

I turned my head, and there it was. Rooted in the ground, one leg raised, beady eye staring back at me.

I blinked. I blinked again.

I went inside.

When I came back out, it was back where she had left it. To the left of the lilac tree, just slightly crooked.

The next day, it was by the sliding glass door.

It was rooted in the planks of the patio, eyes looking in, just beyond the glass.

I scratched my head. Literally scratched my head. Then I went and took a shower.

If my brain was melting, I didn't want my mom to have to deal with my funk too. She'd gone through enough shit. Time to clean things up.

Tomorrow. I'd do the dishes tomorrow.

The next day, the flamingo was in the kitchen. Which honestly kind of pissed me off. It was hard enough getting up the energy to load the dishwasher or find the goddamn soap when the love of my life was . . . not. Life. Not life.

I should have gone to her therapist. I didn't have the words for it. I held my breath, picked up the flamingo, ran back outside, and stuck it in the flowerpot.

After two months, that was my proudest moment.

Fifty yard dash back to the couch.

I set my water bottle on the coffee table and crossed my legs, staring at the door. I wasn't letting it in. Not this time. Fucking bird. What the hell? I didn't need its stupid pink flaking ass. I needed Jane. I needed my goddamn everything.

Two hours. Three hours. Four. Nothing came in the door. Nothing moved across the patio. The flamingo stayed in its pot.

My notebook was on the table. I picked up my pen.

When she
When I
When
When

What was I going to say? There was nothing after. Only me. Nothing more. I threw the pen. I watched it roll across the floor. Nothing mattered. Not without her.

I stayed that way for a long time.

Notebook open in my lap, I finally fell asleep.

I opened my eyes, and the flamingo was there, upright, balanced next to the side table.

A mug of tea steamed on the coaster.

The blanket from my bed was tucked under my chin.

My notebook sat open in my lap.

The pen held my page.

Fuck.

I looked down at the words, scrawled in her handwriting:

When

"When," I said out loud. "When."

I took a deep breath. Stared hard at the flamingo.

"Alrighty then, darling."

I picked up the pen.

When the flamingo appeared, I thought I was going to

Gerald in the Mirror

Erik Grove

Lately, Gerald has been seeing a bird in his EverBox.

"What kind of bird?" Coffee Machine Pete asks, shaking artificial creamer. Shake, shake, shake.

"It's big," Gerald says. "Long legs, you know. Looks right at me. Droopy face. Droopy bird face."

Trier From Accounts splits the skin of an orange with a thumbnail. He's a narrow man. Fastidious. "What are you doing when it sees you?" he asks.

The way he phrases the question (when it sees *you* not when you see *it*)—as if the bird is always there and Gerald only knows when it wants him to know—is unsettling. But the way he meticulously plucks every bit of pith between his fingertips is worse.

"I'm not doing anything," Gerald says. "Normal things," he amends. Who talks about what they *do* in an EverBox? At the *office*?

Trier from Accounts drives his thumb into the orange's center and splits the whole thing apart. "What's *normal*?"

Before Gerald can answer, Coffee Machine Pete says, "For a while I was working my way through cartoon characters. The big-name princesses first obviously. But then all the critter companions, the talking furniture. And the dwarves."

The implications of that expand in the awkward silence that follows.

"It's guilt," Trier from Accounts says. He holds out a piece of orange to Gerald. "Wedge?"

"No thank you," Gerald says and then: "I don't understand."

"Yes, you do. Cut far enough in and we're all just bags of shit and neuro-chemical impulses. It's primal, Gerald. Everyone's hands are bloody in their dreams."

Gerald doesn't know what to say. What is there *to* say?

"I did Stephen Hawking," Coffee Machine Pete says. "Pounded him." He slaps his hands together. "Pound, pound, pound."

"Why?" Gerald asks but he regrets it. He doesn't want to know. Not really. He doesn't want to know any of this, doesn't want to endure the sharp smell of masticated orange, or remember the bird's eyes looking at—no, *through* him. Is Trier from Accounts right? Is it guilt? Is it primal?

"Why did Edmund Hillary summit Everest?" Coffee Maker Pete asks. And then he answers himself. "To bust a nut where no one's ever busted a nut before."

He opens the artificial creamer and drinks it just like that.

Gerald was full grown when EverCorp release EverBox model one. Not like his kids. He grew up in the real world mostly.

He always remembers that the model ones included a lot of instructions and fine print. Secure your surroundings. Do not use near open windows. Photosensitive users take caution: may cause seizures. All of that was resolved with the paralytic spinal taps in the model fours. Now, new EverBoxes have a three-panel cartoon. An androgynous user puts the box on their head, presses the power button in the back, and gives two thumbs up.

"At Last: The World You Deserve," the box used to read.

Gerald opens a customer service ticket with EverCorp. There isn't an option for a judgmental bird, so he selects, "Sponsored Content."

The customer service representative is a girl he knew once at the beach in the yellow light, sand on her feet and freckles. Samantha. "How can I help?" she asks.

"Do you see that bird?"

Gerald points at the bird. It is in the clouds and the reflection of glass.

"I value you, Gerald," the customer service rep Samantha tells him. "And I miss the times we had together. I could have loved you, I think. If you are experiencing unexpected imagery in your EverBox experience, please review your repression presets. Does that answer your question?"

"No," Gerald says. But then: "Yes. Thank you."

She gives him a reference number and asks him if he'd like to take a survey.

He could remember her. He could remember the grit of sand between the suntan lotion on his palms and her bronze shoulders.

Pound, pound, pound.

Instead, he administers the anti-paralytic, pulls out the catheter and feeding tubes, and presses the power button on the back of his EverBox.

His wife, son, and daughter are a tableau. They sit straight with stark white boxes on their heads.

Isn't this the way of things, Gerald thinks. Before the EverBox it was hand screens and before hand screens it was the television. Always some soft static glow in living room windows. It is not an original lament, he thinks, to long for a time when families ate supper at the table, when technology didn't seem so heavy. Kissing sweat off of Samatha and standing up to his knees in the waves, the sky unpoisoned, and his cock, slap, slap, slapping between his thigh and his swimming trunks.

Gerald opens the menu for his repression presets. The EverBox assistant suggests for his demographic he change the level to seven, at least. The algorithm will do the rest.

Trier from Accounts stops at Gerald's desk. His haircut is neat, and his fingernails are trimmed. When he sees him, Gerald still smells oranges.

"Last night, I wrapped an extension cord around your neck," Trier from Accounts says. "And I put my knee between your shoulders here." He reaches around and touches his spine. "I used a timer so I would know. It took three minutes. Just under three minutes. Two minutes and fifty-two seconds. I thought it would take longer."

"I don't want you to tell me that," Gerald says.

"Everyone does it, Gerald. They fuck and they kill. They put on the box, and they do it all. It's only your imagination. It doesn't *matter*."

Gerald wants to say, "It matters to me," and feels foolish immediately. Most of his thoughts make him feel foolish.

Instead, Gerald says, "I have a meeting."

"Jesus doesn't mind, Gerald. God and the Pope, they're in the box too."

Gerald leaves his desk. He goes to the men's room and locks himself into a stall.

Trier from Accounts sends him a message. "We slept together after. It wasn't sexual. It's not always sexual. I didn't want to be alone. Don't you ever want that? To not be alone?"

(*"I could have loved you, I think."*)

Federal regulators put a timer on the EverBox. There were deaths. Liabilities. And there's the economy to consider. After six consecutive hours, full immersion is disabled.

Of course there are workarounds.

Gerald thinks it would be nice to have supper at the table, so he comes home with a spice fried protein bucket and disposable plates.

"What's new?" he asks the children, and his daughter goes through a list of horrors he does not want to hear. Other places, burning. Other people, dying. This is feeling too much. He cannot be responsible for this. He cannot.

He asks his son, and his son says, "I don't know."

He asks his wife, and she says, "Next Door Marty sawed his foot off at the ankle. Fed it into a saw just like that." She tears protein to strips. "He wants the disability. Fucking pathetic."

Gerald tells them about the bird.

"Is it the one from the cereal?" his son asks.

"No," Gerald says. "Which cereal?"

"What color is it?" his daughter asks.

"Red," Gerald says. "No. It fades toward the tips of its feathers. Pink."

"That's a flamenco," his son says.

They all laugh.

"A pink flamingo *means* something, Gerald," his wife says.

"What does it mean?" he asks her.

She slides her index finger through a hole she's made with her other hand. Slide, slide, slide.

"I don't think that's right," Gerald says, and he wonders why things can't simply mean nothing anymore. Why is there always a double entendre, a wink, something lascivious? He wonders if there's something wrong with him, if he should be putting the EverBox on his head and pound, pound, pounding Sleeping Beauty or his wife, Samantha, or Trier from Accounts.

Should he fuck the bird? Is that what it wants?

Why is he like this? Why is he so afraid?

In his EverBox, Gerald prefers to use pre-imagined content. Someone else's dreams. He could make his own experience— the world he "deserves," according to the old ad copy—but what if the world he deserves is disappointing?

Or worse; what if the worst parts of himself seep through? The guilt. The bird. What if his hands are bloody like Trier from Accounts suggests? He doesn't need to be a saint, but he can't trust himself not to be a monster.

Does he resent his wife? Of course he does. Is he disappointed in his children, his job, his everything? Does he want more or different or Samantha and the yellow light? Those are questions better unasked. The unexamined life is safer.

Gerald asks the bird on its legs, its pink flamenco feathers, "What are you?"

The bird is a bird. It cannot tell him what he needs to hear.

Is the bird death, Gerald wonders? A thought so natural it must have been waiting for him. Cut far enough in, isn't everything death? The clock is death. The setting sun is death. The ocean that carries it all away, death, death, death. All the poets and charlatans describing death like parts of an existential elephant no one can really see but everyone knows is there. Always there.

Sex is death. Pound, pound, pounding death.

And Gerald. Gerald in the mirror, he's death too.

Why would he that want that in his EverBox?

Gerald's wife sends him a message. An article about pink flamingos. They are an indicator, a code, for people in the swinging lifestyle, the article explains. Spouse swappers.

"Is this what you want?"

He doesn't reply and she sends him profiles. Pink flamingos near them. Judy and Rick are only 7-minutes away.

Coffee Maker Pete tells Gerald that he has started working his way through his own family tree.

"I found digital photos," he says. "And I fill in the details, you know?"

Pound, pound, pound.

Gerald punches him in the mouth. He makes a fat line in Coffee Maker Pete's kiss.

The office goes into an uproar. People stare. Human resources is engaged.

Trier from Accounts puts his hands on Gerald's shoulders and rubs at the knots. "There you go," he says, smelling always of ascorbic acid. "Now you're getting it. You were made to break bones against the rocks. Inside of your engineered white box is a savage inchoate scream. Let it out, Gerald. The bird needs to fly."

That night, Gerald sends another message to EverBox Customer Service. "I've missed you too."

"It's no different than the EverBox," Gerald's wife tells him while they pack for their first couple date. (Should he bring a change of clothes? For *after*? Should he have a different outfit for the trip home?) "As if you haven't fantasized a hundred different women in there. A thousand maybe."

"No," Gerald says. "I don't know. It's not real."

"What's *real*?" she asks and then, a cruel smile: "Tell me about them."

"I don't want to," he says.

His wife knows this about him, that he is uncomfortable, that he is a lights-out lover. He is not a man that can *grab* or *grope* or *fondle*. Dirty talk catches in his throat. It sounds too profane or childish or clinical.

Cock. Boob. Coitus. His cheeks warm, his eyes dart away.

He knows she thinks it makes him pathetic and he wonders what the world she deserves is like? When she puts on her EverBox, is he ever there?

"You'll fuck a parade of them in your mind, some stranger you saw at the supermarket in yoga pants, but you won't fuck Judy on Pine Terrace with me in the other room?" Gerald's wife asks and she laughs, laughs at him. "Honestly, Gerald, you're more prudish than my *grandfather*."

He is. He knows he is. He doesn't want to summit Everest or wrap an electrical cord tight around anyone's neck. He doesn't *want*.

They leave the kids in their EverBoxes.

"Don't forget your homework," Gerald says and his son's catheter bag fills with fresh, warm piss.

Judy and Rick on Pine Terrace have wine waiting. Rick has very symmetrical teeth and when Judy talks about her day, she says it was "so flustrating."

"We didn't see a pink flamenco out front," Gerald tells them. No one laughs.

"Should we get more comfortable then?" Rick asks and Judy refills their wine.

"Now Rick," Judy says. "Rick, Rick, Rick."

Somehow Gerald and Rick are left on the living room couch while the wives see about something in the kitchen or bathroom or bedroom, and Rick says, "I know this is your first time."

Gerald nods along with his wine glass.

"You're worried," Rick says. "And that's okay. The lifestyle, it isn't for everyone. You need trust. Trust in yourself, trust in your wife, trust in us. Do you trust me?"

Gerald doesn't trust anyone least of all himself.

"No one is going to make you do anything that makes you uncomfortable," Rick says. He smiles. "You're going to be okay." He takes a small bottle of pills from his pocket. "I'm going to take one of these. Do you want one? It will make you go all night long."

Pound, pound, pound.

Gerald sees the bird through the window. It looks through him.

This isn't real, Gerald thinks. I imagined this. I don't want to imagine this. His worst parts seeping through.

When they get home, Gerald takes the EverBox with him to bed. He bypasses the immersion rules. He sleeps beside Trier from Accounts.

He doesn't want to be alone.

Coffee Maker Pete comes by after work.

"I told my Dad," he says. "He disowned me." He falls down crying and Gerald holds him through it, holds Coffee Maker Pete trembling like a little boy that doesn't know that monsters creep back under the bed sooner or later.

"I don't know," Coffee Maker Pete keeps saying. "I don't know . . ."

And Gerald thinks about prudish grandfathers and his throat-caught dirty words. It would be so easy if he was right, if he could put it all back in the EverBox and never talk about it. Judy and Rick on Pine Terrace. Other places, burning. Other people, dying. If it could fit. All the sex and death and

shame locked up tight. God and the Pope are in the box. And
the bird. The silent, watching bird.

But he's not right. He knows that he isn't. He knows it isn't
easy. It's not supposed to be. Sex is a strange, chemical thing.
Dyslexic for love. And sex is falling, spent, onto the August
beach beside Samantha. A beautiful, kinky, terrifying knot
within him that no one else's hands can loosen.

Who does he *want* in the EverBox? Who does he want to
hold and taste and abandon?

Gerald in the mirror.

He'd like to hold him down, bite his lip to copper tang, drag
hands up and down, and fuck Death Himself all night long.

Do they make a pill for that, he wonders.

Customer Service Samantha says, "We're sorry for your frus-
tration."

(*So flustrating.*)

She repeats Gerald's reference number from the ticket
he submitted, and she explains about the glitch. "A limited
number of our users experienced a malfunction in their
repression settings. It seems a subconscious artifact mani-
fested outside of EverCorp standards."

"An artifact?" Gerald repeats.

"A pink flamingo," she says. "Long legs. Droopy face."

"The bird," Gerald says.

"Right," Customer Service Samantha says. "It should never
have been there. Our bad."

The real Samantha grew up. She survived cancer. She never

worked any kind of shitty AI customer service. She deserves to be a better memory, but Gerald doesn't know her. He hasn't seen her outside his EverBox in 20 years.

"We've deposited a generous credit to your EverBox store account," she says.

And then she asks him if he'd like to take a survey.

Gerald removes his EverBox. He takes it into his backyard, and he smashes it into the earth. He finds a hammer in the garage, and he pound, pound, pounds it to shattered nothing.

He goes to Trier from Accounts's apartment. It is small and immaculate and the walls are mandarin.

"I am not a savage, inchoate scream," Gerald says.

Trier nods. "Okay."

"I am quiet and shy and I don't know how to talk about some things."

"Okay," Trier says.

Gerald puts his hand on Trier's cheek. Clean-shaven. Smooth. He kisses him. Like yellow light.

"Is it okay?" Gerald asks.

Trier nods.

Gerald takes his hand. "Come with me," he says, and they go.

Hook & Land

Mark Teppo

MONDAY

The light changes on his console, but Roger barely looks at his display. *Here we go.* Thirty-third call today. He's got the new script down. "Hello," he says into his headset. "My name is Roger. Do you have issues with dampness *down*stairs." He takes the beat, knowing this is his opening. The person on the other end of the call, the lead—the *gillie*, in the parlance of the seventh floor—will be confused by his emphasis. Is he talking about . . . ? "Your basement," Roger says. "Dampness in your basement." Giving them the out. It's not *that* sort of call.

An idle glance at his deck shows a blank caller ID display. His mouth tightens. *Another one?* The leads are getting worse. How can he hook this lead if he doesn't know who he is talking to? Is the gillie in charge of the household? Do they rent? Are they in an apartment?

Ultimately, it doesn't matter. The gillie is in his queue. He's got to land it. Otherwise, the lead counts against him. "With extreme weather on the rise, you can't be too careful," he says, getting back on script. "You and your, uh, your family need a safe—"

"Hey, listen to me."

Roger ignores the voice on the line. He's got to maintain control of the conversation. "—a safe place to shelter, and what better place to shelter than in a subterranean space that will protect you from tornados, hurricanes, firestorms, locust swarms . . ."

There are a dozen more catastrophic disasters in the script, but Roger knows he can trim the list. It's a fresh fisher who makes the mistake of going verbatim on the script. You have to adapt. Feel the tension on the line, know when you've got them hooked. *Which would be easier if I had caller data*, Roger thinks.

Roger works on the seventh floor of the Follyplex Mercantile Exchange, an industrial high-rise on the north side of the river. If there were windows on this floor—and there aren't any, really, except maybe on twelve or above—all they would see is the drainage ponds and the rusted pipes of the reclamation plant. A shit view, which they don't have the time for anyway. There are calls to make. Gills to hook. Quotas to land. Policies to sell.

"No, man. Stop the script. Listen."

Roger pauses.

"You—yeah, you there?" The voice on the phone is breathless. A little incredulous.

"As I was saying—" Roger reaches for his spiral bound script book. He flips it open, flicking through the pages for the script he's supposed to be reading. *Abscess Draining. Adjustment Services. Automobile Repossession. Bad Debt Consolidation.* Yes, here it is. Basement Maintenance and Repair. "—your family needs—"

"It's beautiful, man. I'm telling you. It's the most beautiful thing—"

Roger terminates the call.

The caller ID screen on his console remains blank.

A yellow light comes on, reminding him to categorize the call. There are four options on his deck, marked with tiny icons: the skull, the circle, the right-pointing arrow, and the up arrow. Roger reaches for his deck, but his finger hesitates over the button marked with the skull. If he marks the lead DEAD, the watchers and counters on nine will review the call, verifying the fault wasn't his.

Roger knows the trolls will go to the audio log.

His finger drifts right, over the circle, and stops on the first arrow. He presses it, putting the lead back into his queue. He'll have another chance tomorrow. And the day after. All the way until the close of business on Friday when the queues dump, and the lingering leads become black marks on his tally.

The ready light on his console flashes green. The next lead has been loaded. The caller ID screen fills with data, and Roger taps the "Accept" button on his deck. "Hello, Mrs. Gershwon, it's Roger. How are you doing today? How about downstairs? Any unexpected dampness?"

By the end of his shift—fifty-three calls—he's forgotten all about the one with no caller information. But it's still there, circling in his queue. Waiting for another chance.

☆

TUESDAY

"Hello, this is Roger. I'd like to talk to you today about dampness. The dampness that you don't know is there, downstairs. It lurks—"

"Hey, Roger. Listen to me."

Roger is annoyed at the intrusion. One of the mandatory training sessions focused on leads that wriggled on the line. *Some people will try to interrupt*, the trainer had said to the room of bored seventh-floor fishers. *They'll try to commandeer the call. They think if they can get you to break from the script and interact with them as people—as a real person on the line—you'll realize what you're doing.*

What are we doing? some smartass had asked in the back of the room.

You're hooking leads, the trainer had said. *It's not fancy, and frankly, not all that hard. Your job is to hook 'em in the gills and land them so they can be processed by eight.*

Hook 'em and land 'em. That's the job. The more calls you send upstairs, the better your standing on the boards, and end-of-week pay is based on those rankings. You want to be in the top twenty—that's where everything is green and gold. End up as a bottom feeder, and it's all red. More rocks in that debt load you're carrying.

"You gotta see it, Roger," the caller is babbling. "It's so green and beautiful . . ."

"Look—" Roger notices the caller ID screen on his deck is blank.

"You're never going to get out of there, Roger. It's a lie. You never get off the floor. It doesn't matter how many gillies you hook. There's no way out. Not from there. But I know a way. I've seen it."

Roger leans toward his deck, but he doesn't reach for the button that will terminate the call. "I'm calling about your basement," he says. He's not really listening to what he is saying; his mouth is going through the motions while thoughts race around his head. "If the walls down there are damp, that's the first sign. There's still time if you get to it quick enough."

Who is he talking to? How do they know his name? How do they know about 'gillies' and 'hooks'?

You told him your name, a voice in his head reminds him. It's the first thing you do on a call. Make that connection. First-name basis. *'Hi, I'm Roger. Won't you invite me in?'*

"I know you don't have a lot of time," the voice continues. "The calls are logged. You've got to keep moving. Keep landing. You can't listen to me. Not for long. 'Cause if you're listening, you're not talking, and they want you talking, don't they?"

Roger nods unconsciously. He rises from his chair and peers over the walls of the cubicle farm that breaks up the seventh floor into eighty-four identical squares. "I'm sorry," he says. "The homeowner isn't available right now? When do you expect them to be back?"

"Don't toss me out your queue, Roger. I need to tell you what I've seen. You've got to believe me!"

"Not until tomorrow?" Roger sees that Terry, in the next cube over, is watching him. His mouth is moving; he's on the second step of the Cutlery Upgrade portion of the kitchen makeover script. Terry quirks an eyebrow into a question, and Roger responds with a hand gesture that could mean a lot of things, but among fishers, it means 'letting line out so the gillie doesn't realize they are hooked.'

"I'd be delighted to talk to the head of your household tomorrow," Roger says. "In the meantime, you should spend some time in your basement. Are there spots that feel more damp than others? No, I don't expect you to know now. That's why I'm asking you to check after we're done talking today. I want to know what your basement feels like."

"Don't tell anyone about me, Roger," his caller says. "This is our secret. Trust *me*. I'm trusting *you*."

The call light on his console winks once, twice, and then turns orange. He's been on the call too long. "All right," Roger says. "Let's talk tomorrow." He ends the call. His finger hesitates over the decision buttons. He can't skull it. QA'll listen to the audio. They're hear everything.

Roger stabs the follow-up button again, putting this call back into his queue. He stares at his console for a minute, wondering what he's done. What he's going to do about this call. He only has a few more days before it dumps.

What was he talking about?

WEDNESDAY

"I'm going to get the steak knives this quarter." Terry has done the math, and he likes the numbers. "I'm up three percent right now, and the quarter's over at the end of the week. There's no way anyone can catch me."

Roger has been staring at the swirl of fake creamer that won't dissolve in his watery coffee. He isn't thinking about numbers or the board or the end of the quarter. Friday afternoon. The bell rings. The queues get dumped. Tallies are made. How many hooked? How many landed? How many left behind? Roger isn't thinking about any of that.

Terry, however, oh, this is all Terry is thinking about.

"I thought you were stacking gillies," he says. "Waiting for the back half of the week to land them all. But man, I don't think that's it."

"What?" Roger pulls his attention away from the swirl of his coffee. "What are talking about?"

"You, man, you're about to fall off the board."

Roger blinks and focuses on Terry. "The board?" He looks out the floor-to-ceiling window of the break room. Mounted on the far wall of the floor is the board, the electronic display that tracks their lives: number of calls, depth of their queue, sales sent upstairs, and—at the end of the row in pixelated red—the ones that got away.

It's not as simple as Terry thinks it is—you don't add the money number to the success rate and subtract the deficit. No, there's an algorithm behind it, a complicated calculation that is tweaked and optimized and squeezed by analysts farther upstairs. What the fishers see is an order on the board: first to last. Steak knives to debt accumulation.

And Terry is right about two things, though: his name is at the top, and Roger's isn't.

"I've—I've had a run of..." Roger doesn't finish. Terry doesn't care. Management won't care. The fishers fish. They hook and land. They send the gillies upstairs to be processed. And if you can't make quota, you don't stay on the seventh floor.

"Steak knives," Terry says. "It's going to be so awesome."

An hour later, when the call comes round in his queue, Roger lowers his head and listens. He listens as long as he can.

THURSDAY

Roger missed his usual shuttle from the depot by three minutes, which means waiting twenty-two minutes for the next ride. He'll be late to his desk, which means he'll have to submit a request to voluntarily forgo his morning and afternoon breaks in order to meet the call minimum. He needs to make quota today. Terry is right; he's been off the last few days, and the results are showing on the board.

Roger waits in the terminal, fretting. Worrying. Trying to get his head in the game. Get the gillies on the line. Hook 'em. Land 'em. Make the numbers. Get off the bottom.

But, in the back of his mind, the dream lingers.

It was the reason he had trouble getting out of bed this morning. The reason he wasn't sure where he was when he woke. *It's so beautiful and green*, the caller had said. *It's right outside the door. I can see it.*

The data scroller at the terminal says air quality is hazardous. Whatever is on fire is still burning. *Wear masks. Stay indoors.* Roger and the rest of the workers waiting for the shuttle don't even notice the warnings. They're all the same, anymore.

It's so beautiful and green.

When the shuttle reaches the station beneath the Follyplex Mercantile Exchange, Roger is greeted with a sign that the elevators aren't working. An arrow directs him to the stairwell at the end of the hall. He's out of breath by the third floor. By the fifth, he realizes he's going to be late enough that both of his breaks won't cover his absence. He'll have to voluntarily forgo lunch as well.

He pauses on the seventh-floor landing. Lunch is twenty-seven minutes. If he gives it up, he gives up all that time. It's a checkbox on the form. They use the same principle when they are fishing. All or nothing. You're in or you're out. There's no percentages. Winning or losing.

Roger looks at the stairs that continue past the seventh floor. *It's on the tenth floor*, the caller had said. *At the end of the hall. The door marked with the yellow star.*

But how do I get there? he had asked. *My key card only works for seven.*

The stairs, the caller had said. *Take the stairs. The door on ten isn't locked.*

Roger knows he is late. His queue is filling. His quota isn't filling. He has to get to his desk. He has to hook and land. He should be on the clock.

The door isn't locked.

"A few minutes," Roger whispers. "I have a few minutes."

He turns and starts up the stairs.

FRIDAY

The day begins with a blue light. A minute before the queues open, they all hear the same message from Management. "End of Quarter extension," the voice says into every headset. "You have two more days to fish. There are new scripts for the weekend. New leads to hook. Bonuses are available. Engagement is expected. Closure is rewarded. No action is required. Your presence will be recorded."

"Shit," Terry says in the next cubicle. Two more days of fishing means his steak knives could be in jeopardy.

Two more days means Roger might not end up a bottom-feeder.

But that's not what Roger is thinking about. He's thinking about the call still circling in his queue. The one he hasn't landed. The one that hasn't gotten away.

His first call arrives. The caller ID screen tells him what needs to know. Roger presses the button on his console. "Hi, my name is Roger, and I'm calling to talk to you about your pet's hair loss."

On the tenth floor, behind the door marked with the yellow star.

SATURDAY

"Have you ever thought about—" Roger stops himself, but not soon enough.

"Thought about what?"

Roger sees the way Terry looks at him. He knows what Terry is thinking. He hasn't been sleeping, and what sleep he does manage to steal is filled with color and light. Green and yellow. Stars and clouds. He wants that dream, even as he hates it. He knows it can't be true. *Air quality hazardous. Wear your mask. Stay indoors.* Roger fidgets with his cup—his fifth of the day, black, no powdered creamer. There's a hum in his ears. A persistent, nagging buzz of an impulse—a desire—that won't go away. *So green and beautiful.*

"Steak knives," he says, forcing all the other thoughts away. "I was thinking about steak knives."

Terry narrows his eyes. "I think about them all the time," he says.

"Yeah, but what comes after that?"

"What do you mean?"

"You win the steak knives. Okay, but what about next quarter?"

Terry doesn't understand. "I win them again," he says as matter-of-factly as if he was talking about breathing or walking.

"Not the knives. Come on, Terry, when was the last time you had something that actually required a knife to eat?"

"That's not the point."

"That's exactly the point," Roger counters. "Isn't there something . . . something more?"

"Like what?"

"I don't know."

"A promotion? Like getting off this floor and moving up in the company?"

On the tenth floor. At the end of the hall.

"Sure," Roger says. His vision blurs. The light in the break room is too bright. Too white.

Terry grins. "End of the year, man. That's the big win. End of the year. I can turn all those stupid knives in for a promo." He leans closer. "But you ain't going to make it, Roger. Not with your numbers bouncing on the bottom. Even with these two extra days. You can't catch me."

"I don't know that I want to," Roger hears himself say. He lifts his face and stares into the light. The white light. The hard light. He finds himself wishing it were a different color. Softer. Warmer. More . . . more yellow.

SUNDAY

The call is the fourth one in his queue. The voice is weaker, but Roger recognizes it. He hears it all night now, whispering in his ear when he tries to sleep. "Last chance," the voice says. "For both of us. We got lucky with the extension, but after today's shift, I'm out of your queue. You know this."

"I know," Roger whispers. The dump is coming. Any calls left at end of business get shuffled to a different fisher, and Roger gets deficits on his tally. It won't show on the board, but Management knows. The algorithm knows. This fisher can't hook. He has trouble landing. Why are we wasting good gillies on him?

"You've got to come up here. At the end of the hall. It's the only chance, for both of—"

The light on his console turns blue. Struggling to breath, Roger reaches for his console and presses the button to accept the interruption. "Yes?"

"This is an automated reminder from Follyplex Mercantile Exchange Incorporation. Your quota has not been met. You have . . . six . . . hours to fill your quota. Failure to fill your quota will result in a performance devaluation and a payroll deduction. Should this deduction be greater than your allowance, it will be added to your contract. With this change to your contract, Follyplex Mercantile Exchange Incorporation may, at its sole discretion, reevaluate the lending rate applied to your contract and adjust it in accordance with current market rates. For your information, the current market rate is—"

Roger rips off his headset, reducing the voice to a metallic chatter. Like a piece of metal caught in a duct somewhere. He can't end the blue-light call. Management tracks his console activity. If he ends the call without hearing all of it, they will know.

Roger looks across the cubicle farm of the seventh floor. His eyes glaze over the boards—Terry's name at the top; his name . . . it's doesn't matter where his name is. Roger looks at the door with the green sign over it. The stairwell door. The elevators still aren't working. Nothing is working.

"Hey! What are you doing?" Terry peers over the cubicle wall they share. "There are calls in the queue." He notices the blue light on Roger's console. "You've got a—"

"I'm going for a walk," Roger says.

He walks down the aisle between cubicles. At the end of the row, he turns and walks along the outer wall, beneath the boards. All the way to the door with the green sign. He pushes it open and walks away from his cubicle and the eighty-three others just like it. Away from the fishbowl break room where the light is too bright. Too white.

He walks up the stairs, past the landing of the eighth floor. Past the ninth. All the way to the tenth.

The stairwell door is unlocked, like his caller said it would be. Like it was the other day when he snuck up here—breath in his throat, heart hammering in his chest.

He opens the door and walks down the hall. Past unmarked doors. *Sixteen, seventeen, eighteen.* This is as far as he got last time. As far as he would let himself go. At the eighteenth door, his nerve failed, and he turned back. He had to get to his desk. He had to get on the queue. Take some calls. Hook and land some gillies. He had a job to do.

But now, he keeps walking. *Nineteen. Twenty.* He can see the door. He can see the yellow star on it.

Roger reaches the door at the end of the hall. He tries the latch. It isn't locked. Just like the stairwell door.

It's the only chance, for both of us . . .

Roger hooks his hand around the latch and opens the door.

GROVE

Erik Grove is a writer, writing teacher, long distance runner, and little dog wrangler doing things in Portland, OR. He enjoys tacos, robots, and using italics for *emphasis*. You can find his work in *Nightmare, Escape Pod, Buckman Journal*, prior volumes of *Space Cocaine*, and other esteemed places like his mom's refrigerator.

Visit www.erikgrove.com for links to his published work, information on editorial and mentoring services, upcoming readings and appearances, and sundry writerly shenanigans.

LUFF

Cody grew up listening to stories in his grandfather's barber shop as he shined shoes, stories told to him at bedsides and on front porches, and deep in his father's favorite woods.

Cody is a founding member of Working Title Writers (https://www.workingtitle.us/) and his debut novel, *Ration*, was released by Apex Book Company in 2019.

MESSERSMITH-GLAVIN

Lara Messersmith-Glavin is an author, educator, and performer based in Portland, Oregon. You can find both her nonfiction and her speculative work in dozens of journals and anthologies, including *Winding Paths: a Playable Reading Experience* (Demagogue Press: 2023). Her book of essays, *Spirit Things* (UA Press: 2022), won Finalist for the Willa Cather Literary Award and the Sarton Women's Book Award and was recently released as an audiobook. Her fantasy novel *Ruiner* is due out on AK Press in 2025.

McCOLLOUGH

A.W.McCollough writes science fiction, fantasy, and horror from his workshop in the Pacific Northwest. His work tends to describe unfortunate things happening to relatable protagonists, often involving magic or robots. Sometimes both.

His work is available at www.worlds.working title.us.

NAKAMURA

Remy Nakamura is a writer of dark and weird fiction. You can find his stories in *Escape Pod*, *Pseudopod*, and a number of anthologies. He is a graduate of the Clarion West Writers Workshop and currently serves on the Science Fiction & Fantasy Writers Association (SFWA) Board as a Director at Large. Remy grew up in Greece, Japan, and the San Francisco Bay Area. He lives in Portland, Oregon, where he spends as much time as possible getting cold, wet, and muddy.

RISTAU

Kate Ristau is an author, folklorist, and the Executive Director of Willamette Writers. She is the author of three middle grade series, *Clockbreakers, Mythwakers*, and *Wylde Wings,* and the young adult series, *Shadow Girl.* You can read her essays in *The New York Times* and *The Washington Post.*

Meet her online at Kateristau.com.

SHERRILL

Jeb R. Sherrill has an oddly disjointed background. Having stumbled through everything from performing stage magic and kinetic juggling on French television and in Las Vegas casinos, to teaching martial arts and circus techniques, to competitive sabre fencing, film and stage acting, dance, songwriting, and his ongoing stint as a popular YouTube personality, Jeb has the ADD of a 10 year old. Writing, however, has remained his greatest passion since early childhood, having also written a barrage of short stories and poetry.

Pinning down his style is difficult, however. His liquid, psychotropic images, philosophical undertones and pure unabashed strangeness have made fans across the Fantasy and Science Fiction spectrum. Best known for insane worlds, over the top characters and sometimes heady subject matter, his work may not be for the faint of heart, but reading it is always an adventure. He considers himself to be a fantasticst and a writer of fairy tales for adults.

TEPPO

Mark Teppo divides his time between Portland and Sumner, and he tends to navigate by local bookstore positioning. He writes historical fiction, fantasy, speculative fiction, and horror, and has published more than a dozen novels. If he's writing a mystery, he's pretending to be Harry Bryant.

He also runs Underland Press, an independent publishing house.

You can learn more about him at www.markteppo.com, or follow him on Instagram (@mark.teppo). He's rarely on Twitter anymore.

More Stuff

There's a mailing list. Sign up!

  http://spacecocaine.com

Mostly it'll be used to alert you to future shipments of *Space Cocaine.*

Fancy Doodle Page

Space Cocaine 5 premiered in 2024. This is the page where the authors made their marks should you have been lucky enough to have been in the same room with them.